BIBLE
PICTURE STORIES

BIBLE PICTURE STORIES
From the Old and New Testaments

as told by Carol Mullan
illustrated by Gordon Laite

 ®GOLDEN PRESS
Western Publishing Company, Inc.
Racine, Wisconsin

0-307-10496-6
Sixth Printing, 1979

Soon it will rain so hard that the whole world will be covered with water. Noah and his family and all the animals will be safe in this boat called an ark.

Gen. 7:13-23

Jacob has made a fine coat of many colors to give to his son Joseph. Joseph knows that his father loves him very much.

Gen. 37:3

Joseph has been in Egypt for many years. He is very happy to see his younger brother, Benjamin, and his ten older brothers again. They are glad to see him, too.

Gen. 43-45

Pharaoh's daughter has found baby Moses' basket.
When she opens it, he cries. She feels sorry for the
baby and decides to take care of him. Moses' sister,
Miriam, watches nearby and is glad.

Exod. 2:1-10

When Moses holds his rod over the sea, God makes a wide, dry path so that Moses' people can get to the other side. The wicked Pharaoh and his soldiers will not catch them now.

Exod. 14:5-29

God gave Moses many laws to help the people to live better. Moses carries some of the laws, written on two stone tablets, down from Mount Sinai. We call these laws the Ten Commandments.

Exod. 31:18; 32:15-16; 34:1-4, 27-28

Naomi and Ruth have come to Bethlehem to live. Ruth gathers corn and barley in the fields of Boaz so that she and Naomi will have something to eat. Boaz tells his men to leave many sheaves of barley for her.

Ruth 1:11-2:18

God has told Samuel the prophet to choose a new king
to rule over Israel. Samuel sends for Jesse's youngest
son, David the shepherd boy. He will be the new king.

1 Sam. 16:1-12

Commanded by God, ravens bring bread and meat to Elijah. He gets water to drink from the brook that runs near the cave where he is hiding.

1 Kings 17:1-6

The beautiful and good Queen Esther goes to see the king. She wants to persuade him to save her people, the Jews, from the evil Haman. The king loves his wife, and he listens to her. The Jews will be safe.

Esther 2:16-7:10

Lying in a manger, baby Jesus looks up at the shepherds who have come to Bethlehem to see him. Mary, his mother, and Joseph, her husband, smile at Jesus.

Luke 2:15-16

Jesus listens to the men in the temple. Although he is only twelve years old, he knows he must learn many things. The men are surprised at how well he understands what they say.

Luke 2:41-47

Peter's mother-in-law is one of the sick people whom Jesus heals. As he takes her hand and helps her up, her fever goes away, and she is well again.

Matt. 8:14-17; Mark 1:29-34; Luke 4:38-40

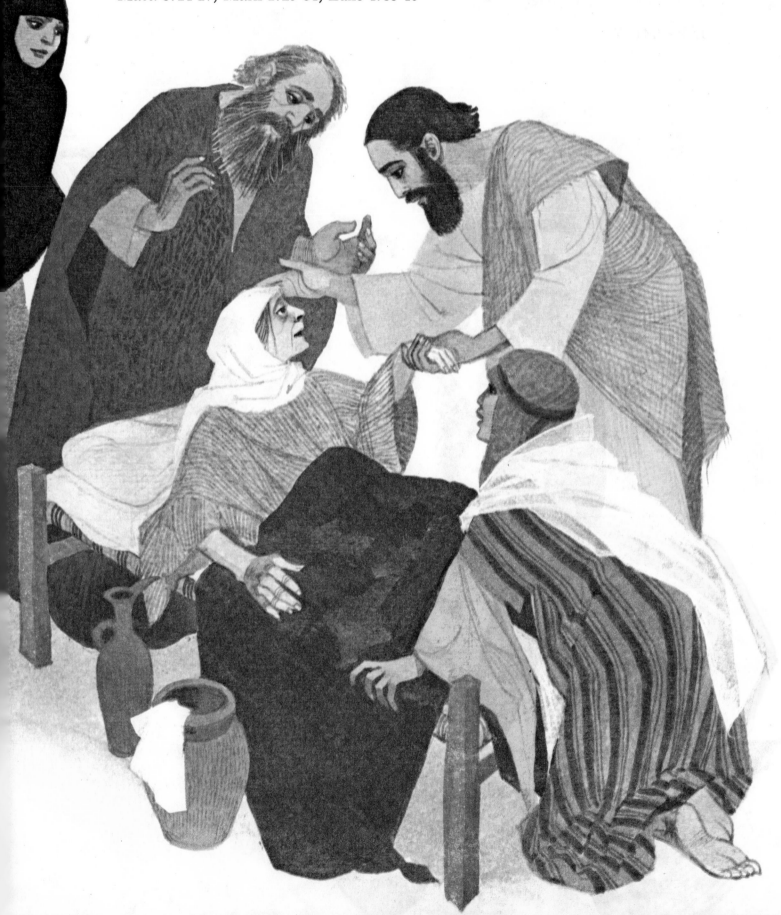

A little boy shares his dinner with the people who came to listen to Jesus. Jesus blesses the five little loaves of bread and the two small fish, and then his twelve disciples pass them out to the people. Everyone has all he wants to eat.

Matt. 14:14-21; Mark 6:34-44; Luke 9:11-17; John 6:5-13

Jesus rides into Jerusalem on the back of a young ass. He is going to the feast of the Passover. Many people spread cloth and branches in his path and shout with joy when they see him.

Matt. 21:1-9; Mark 11:1-10; Luke 19:29-38; John 12:12-15

Unaware that Jesus will soon be betrayed by Judas,
Peter, James, and John sleep peacefully. Not far away,
Jesus asks his heavenly Father to help him.

Matt. 26:36-46; Mark 14:32-42; Luke 22:39-47

Standing outside the tomb where he was buried, Jesus speaks to Mary Magdalene. How happy she is to see that he is alive again. Now he will live forever.

Mark 16:9; John 20:11-17; Rev. 1:18